*Railway Series, No. 25*

# DUKE THE LOST ENGINE

by

## THE REV. W. AWDRY

with illustrations by
GUNVOR & PETER EDWARDS

HEINEMANN · LONDON

William Heinemann Ltd
Michelin House
81 Fulham Road
London
SW3 6RB

LONDON MELBOURNE AUCKLAND

First published 1970
Copyright © William Heinemann Ltd 1970
Reprinted 1992
ISBN 0 434 92802 X

Printed and bound in Great Britain by
William Clowes Ltd, Beccles and London

# Foreword

DEAR FRIENDS,

An engine lost in the South American jungle was found after 30 years. A tree had grown through its chimney and hornets nested in its firebox. When mended it gave good service for 30 more years.

"The Duke" was lost too; not in the jungle but in his own shed which a landslide had buried. Not long ago he was dug out and mended. His own railway had been pulled up, so he is now at the Thin Controller's.

THE AUTHOR

"Duke" looks like a real engine called PRINCE. You can see PRINCE running on his own railway at Portmadoc in Wales.

"Small Railway Engines" can be seen at Ravenglass in Cumberland.

# Granpuff

ONCE upon a time three little engines lived in their own little shed on their own little railway. Duke was brown, Falcon blue, and Stuart green.

Duke was the oldest. He had been the first engine on the line, and named after the Duke of Sodor. He was proud of this and wanted everything "just so". Whenever the others did anything they shouldn't, he would say, "That would never suit His Grace."

Other engines came and went, but Duke outlasted them all. Stuart and Falcon used to call him Granpuff.

Duke was fond of them, and tried to keep them in order. They were fond of him, too, as he was so wise and kind, but they did get tired of hearing about His Grace. Sometimes they would wink at each other and chant solemnly:

> "Engines come and engines go,
> Granpuff 'goes on' for ever!"

"You impertinent scallywags," Duke would say indignantly. "Whatever are young engines coming to nowadays?"

"Never mind, Granpuff. We're only young once."

"Well, you'd better mind; unless you want to end up like No. 2."

"Ooooh! Granpuff. Whatever happened?"

"No. 2," said Duke, "was American, and very cocky. He rode roughly and often came off the rails. I warned him to be careful.

"'Listen, Bud,' he drawled. 'In the States we don't care a dime for a few spills.'

"'We do here,' I said, "but he just laughed.

"But he didn't laugh when the Manager took away his wheels, and said he was going to make him useful at last."

"Why? W—W—What did he do?"

"He turned him into a pumping engine. That's what. He's still there, behind our shed."

Stuart and Falcon were unusually good for several days!

Stuart and Falcon became Useful Engines, and all three were happy together for many years.

But hard times came, the mines closed one by one, and the engines had little to do.

At last, their line was closed and people came to buy the engines.

"We'll take Stuart and Falcon," they said; but no one wanted Duke. They thought him too old.

"Cheer up, Granpuff!" called Stuart, as they went away. "We'll find a nice railway, and then you can come and keep us in order!"

They all laughed bravely, but not one of them thought it would ever come true.

Duke's Driver and Fireman oiled and greased him. They sheeted him snugly, and said good-bye. They had to go away and find work.

Duke was alone, locked up in the shed.

"Where's His Grace?" he wondered. "It's not like him to forget me."

But His Grace had been killed in the War, and the new Duke, a boy, hadn't heard of his Little Engine.

"Oh, well," said Duke to himself. "I'll go to sleep. It'll help to pass the time."

Years passed. Winter torrents washed soil from the hills over the shed. Trees and bushes grew around. You wouldn't have known a shed was there, let alone a little engine asleep inside it.

Have you guessed about Stuart and Falcon? Yes, you're quite right. They came to the Thin Controller's Railway. He gave them new coats and new names. Stuart became Peter Sam, and Falcon Sir Handel. They prefer their new names.

That was a long time ago, but they never forgot Granpuff, and often talked about him when alone.

They were excited to hear that the Duke was coming to Skarloey's and Rheneas' 100th birthday; but most disappointed with the Duke who actually came. For he was only a man. . . .

But we must say no more, or we'll spoil the next story.

# Bulldog

EVER since Skarloey and Rheneas had their 100th birthday, Peter Sam had been worried. He kept on saying that the real Duke never came.

"Rubbish!" said Duncan. "Of course he was real!"

"All the same," Peter Sam persisted, "he wasn't *our* Duke."

"Our Duke," said Sir Handel, "is an engine."

"You're as bad as he is. *All* 'engine Dukes' were scrapped. Ask Duck."

"Duck doesn't know everything," Skarloey put in quietly. "Tell us about him, you two."

Here is one of the stories that Peter Sam and Sir Handel told about Granpuff.

It happened when Sir Handel was new to the line. Now, have you remembered that in those days he was called Falcon, and painted blue?

You have? Now we can begin.

The Manager came to see him one day and said he was pleased with his work, so far. "Now, Falcon", he went on, "you must learn the 'Mountain Road'. . . ."

"Yes please, Sir," said Falcon, excited.

". . . So, tomorrow you shall go 'double-heading' on it with Duke. He'll explain everything."

Falcon didn't like this. He thought Duke was a fuss-pot, and a regular old fuddy-duddy.

Duke's train was one for holiday-makers. He called it "The Picnic".

Falcon was ready when Duke arrived. Duke drew forward beside him. "Listen," he said. "The 'Mountain Road' is difficult. You take the train and I'll couple in front."

"No," said Falcon, "I'll lead. How can I learn the road with you lumbering ahead, blocking the view?"

"Suit yourself," said Duke shortly, "but never mind the view. Attend to the track."

"LOOK AT THE TRACK," he puffed again, on starting, "Never mind the view."

"Fuss-pot, Fuss-pot," puffed Falcon, on starting. "Fud-dy dud-dy, Fud-dy dud-dy, Fud-dy dud-dy!"

They rattled through the first tunnel, looped round, recrossed the river and entered the second, climbing all the time. Their speed grew slower and slower.

"Don't dawdle! Don't dawdle!" urged Falcon.

"No hurry, no hurry," puffed Duke stolidly.

The tunnel was curved and pitch dark. Falcon felt stifled. He wanted to get out.

Presently the light grew. Two ribbons of track appeared ahead in the gloom.

"Watch the track! Watch the track!" warned Duke.

"Fuss-pot! Fuss-pot!" scoffed Falcon.

The tunnel mouth grew larger and larger till at last they burst into the sunshine.

The line here swung sharply right. It was laid on a ledge cut in the hillside. Below lay the valley up which they had come. Track and buildings looked tiny, like toys.

No one quite knows what happened next.

Duke said there must have been something on the track and Falcon hadn't kept a good look-out.

Falcon said he was dazzled, so how could he keep a good look-out?

Anyway, their coaches had barely cleared the tunnel when Falcon lurched. His front wheels, derailed, crunched over sleepers and ballast. He came to rest with one wheel uncomfortably near the edge.

Duke had saved Falcon. Now he held on grimly with locked wheels and taut couplings.

"Young idiot!" he hissed. "Stop it! I can't hold you if you shake."

Falcon tried hard to stop shuddering.

Quickly, Duke's Driver and Fireman chocked his wheels, and strengthened the coupling between the two engines.

"Thank you!" said Duke. "Now I'll manage."

With Duke secure, the two crews, helped by a Platelayer, propped up Falcon's front end. They were looking forward to a rest when Duke began "wheeshing" in an alarming way.

His Fireman ran to his cab.

"Water!" he cried. "We want water, quickly."

The Platelayer's cottage stood nearby. He explained to his wife, and the passengers borrowed jugs, buckets, kettles, saucepans—anything in fact which would hold water.

They formed a chain from the well to the engine, and passed them from hand to hand.

The Fireman, meanwhile, reduced his fire, and anxiously watched the gauge.

It was hot and tiring work, for Duke needed many gallons; but at last the Fireman shouted cheerfully, "We're winning! Don't weaken!" And they all set to work again with a will.

They cheered again when the Breakdown Gang arrived. They showed other passengers how to help them lever Falcon back to the rails.

The Manager was at the Top Station. He said he was sorry about the accident, and thanked the passengers for their help.

"Not at all," they said. "We admired the way you put things right, and enjoyed the adventure."

"They thanked Duke and his crew for preventing a nasty accident.

"Your Duke," they said, "is a hero. He stood firm like a bulldog, and just *wouldn't* let go."

Falcon said, "Thank you" too. "I don't know why you bothered after I'd been so rude."

"Oh, well!" replied Duke. "You'd just had a new coat of paint. It would have been a pity if you'd rolled down the mountain and spoilt it. That would never have suited His Grace."

# You Can't Win!

DUKE's "Picnic" was a train for summer visitors. It was his special train. Many people came year after year, just to see him.

He always pulled it even if he felt poorly. "I mustn't disappoint my friends," he would say. "That would never suit His Grace."

The morning run gave no trouble. He took his passengers up the line, and stopped anywhere they wanted. He and his Driver knew all the best places for picnics.

"Peep, pip, peep!" he whistled as they waved goodbye. "Please don't be late when I come back. We might miss the boat, and that would never do."

One day Duke felt poorly at the end of his first "Picnic" journey. He had been short of steam, and was glad of a rest before starting back. His Driver and Fireman had just finished cleaning his tubes, when Stuart bustled in.

"Hullo, Granpuff! Are you short of puff?"

"Nothing of the sort. Routine maintenance."

"Tell you what, Granpuff. You're getting old. You need to take care. We'll have to keep you in order, or one day you'll break down."

"Humph," said Duke. "That'll be the day! You keep me in order! Impudence!"

He puffed away, hooshing crossly from his draincocks.

Duke couldn't stay cross for long. It was a lovely evening. All the picnic parties were ready. The coaches ran well, and they lost no time anywhere. "Couldn't be better! Couldn't be better!" he chuntered happily.

They began to climb. The work was harder, but Duke didn't mind. "I've plenty of steam," he panted. "We'll be up in a couple of puffs."

He needed more than that, though. His puffs changed to wheezes. "It's not so easy! It's not so easy! My old valves *would* start 'blowing' now; but I'll manage. I'll manage!"

But the leaks became worse, and soon he was "Hoooochrooooochshing" hoarsely with escaping steam.

Duke's Driver examined him carefully at the next station while the Guard went to telephone. Anxious passengers gathered round.

"Two engines are coming," the Guard reported. "With luck we'll be away in 15 minutes. You'll easily catch your boat."

Falcon buffered up in front. "Poor old Granpuff," he hooshed importantly. "What a shame you've broken down!"

"Peep, peep, pip, peep! This is the Day!" whistled Stuart cheekily. He was coupled on behind.

"Peep, pip, peep? Are you ready?" whistled Falcon.

"Peep, peep, peep! Yes I am!" replied Stuart, and away they went.

Falcon had left his train at the Middle Station. Arrived there, the cavalcade split up. Falcon went down to the Port with Duke's "Picnic", while Stuart headed Falcon's train with Duke coupled behind.

Stuart was excited. "Fancy me rescuing Granpuff! This is the Day! This is the Day! This is the Day!" he chortled gleefully.

"Poor Granpuff," he thought. "He's much too old. We'll have to keep him in order now. Kindly but firmly; that's it. We'll allow him to have runs sometimes, but Falcon and I'll do the real work. Granpuff'll be cross, but we can't help that."

"Poor old engine! Poor old engine!" he puffed kindly.

Duke was by no means crippled. His valves sounded worse than they were. He could have kept his train, but his Driver said, "No. Our passengers will only be worried."

Duke agreed. He didn't want to spoil their day.

He listened to Stuart chortling, and smiled. He and his Driver had their own joke ready.

At first, they used just enough steam to keep moving; but the last half-mile was uphill.

"Now!" said his Driver. He advanced the Regulator, and Duke responded with a will. He puffed and roared as though the whole train's weight was on his buffers.

People heard the noise from far away. They ran to see what was happening.

At the Works Station Duke uncoupled and went along the loop to the water-tank.

A boy on the platform asked, "Why were there two engines on this train, Daddy? It's most unusual."

"It is," said his father, "but today was different. Stuart broke down, you see, and they had to call Duke out to help him. Duke had a hard job, too, by the sound of it."

"Well, for crying out loud!" exclaimed Stuart. He vanished in a cloud of steam.

Duke wheezed alongside. "Poor old engine!" he chuckled. "Its no good, Stuart; you can't win!"

# Sleeping Beauty

DUKE's story soon spread. The engines told Mr Hugh; Mr Hugh told the Thin Controller; the Thin Controller told the Owner; the Owner told His Grace; His Grace told the Small Controller; the Small Controller told the Thin Clergyman, and the Thin Clergyman told the Fat one.

That is why, one morning, the two clergymen and the Small Controller were looking at maps.

"Our railway," said the Small Controller, "is laid on the bed of the old one, but swings round to end at the road south of that village. The old line kept straight on. It went north of the village and then to the mountains. The maps show the 'Works' at the Old Station. If Duke is anywhere, he's there."

"Are you writing another book, Sir?"

"Yes," said the Thin Clergyman, "but not about you!" He smiled at their downcast faces. "Cheer up!" he went on. "It's about a nice old engine who is lost; but, if you're good, the artist might put you in the pictures."

"Oooooh! Thank you, Sir."

So the clergyman told them about Duke, and Falcon, and Stuart. "So, you see," he continued, "poor Duke was left alone. . . ."

Three Small Engines sighed sympathetically.

". . . and we want to find him, and mend him, and make him happy again. Your Controller wants to help, but he can't if you're naughty."

Three Small Engines promised to be as good as gold!

The three men spent days and days at the Old Station.

They came up every morning on Bert's train. He always whistled "Good luck!" as they walked up the track, but they had nothing in the evening except scratches and torn clothes. They wouldn't give up, though. "Duke's there, somewhere," they said.

The Fat Clergyman found him in the end. Scrambling over a hillock, he trod on something which wasn't there, crashed through a hole and landed, legs astride, on Duke's saddletank.

"Our Sleeping Beauty himself!" he shouted.

The Thin Clergyman and the Small Controller peeped through the hole above.

"Excuse me," enquired Duke. "Are you a Vandal? Driver told me Vandals break in and smash things."

The Fat Clergyman ruefully felt his bruises. "Bless you, no!" he laughed. "I'm quite respectable. I dropped in because I couldn't find your door," and he told Duke about Falcon and Stuart.

"So they *did* remember," said Duke softly; then, "Does His Grace approve?"

"Yes, he's coming."

"To see me? How kind! And I'm all dirty! That will never do. Please clean me."

So they set to work, and by the time the Small Controller had fetched His Grace, Duke was the cleanest of anyone in the shed.

Early next morning Mike brought Workmen and tools. They enlarged the Fat Clergyman's hole, lifted Duke out, and put him on a "low-loader" to take him away by road.

"I'd be ashamed," Duke protested, "to travel by road It's—it's—it's undignified."

"I'm sorry, Duke," said His Grace, "but the Small Railway has no suitable trucks."

Duke gave in then, but so many people came out and greeted him that he felt better. "So they still remember me," he thought happily.

Donald was waiting with a flat truck. Everyone cheered when Duke was lifted onto it, and still more when he started along the Big Railway on the last stage of his journey to his new home.

Peter Sam and Sir Handel were on "early turn". They peeped out of the shed. "He's there!" they whispered, "Shsh! Shsh! Shsh!"

Duke opened his eyes. "You woke me," he grumbled. "In my young days engines were..."

"... seen and not heard, Granpuff. Remember?"

"I remember," said Duke, "two idle good-for-nothings called Falcon and Stuart. ..."

"Good for you, Granpuff! We're glad you've come. We can keep you in order now."

"Keep *me* in order! Impertinence! Be off!"

The pair chuffed away, well content.

"Impudent scallywags, "murmured Duke; but his old eyes twinkled, and for the first time in years he smiled as he dozed in the sun.